To Gary, Alex, and all dads
who give lots of hugs

Thanks to Lee and Emma

Margaret K. McElderry Books
An imprint of Simon & Schuster Children's Publishing Division
1230 Avenue of the Americas, New York, New York 10020
Copyright © 2005 by Karen Katz
All rights reserved, including the right of reproduction in whole or in part in any form.
Book design by Lee Wade
The text for this book is set in Bembo.
The illustrations for this book are rendered in collage, gouache, and colored pencils.
Manufactured in China
10 9 8 7 6 5
CIP data for this book is available from the Library of Congress.
ISBN 0-689-87771-4

daddy hugs 1*2*3

by karen katz

MARGARET K. MCELDERRY BOOKS
NEW YORK LONDON TORONTO SYDNEY

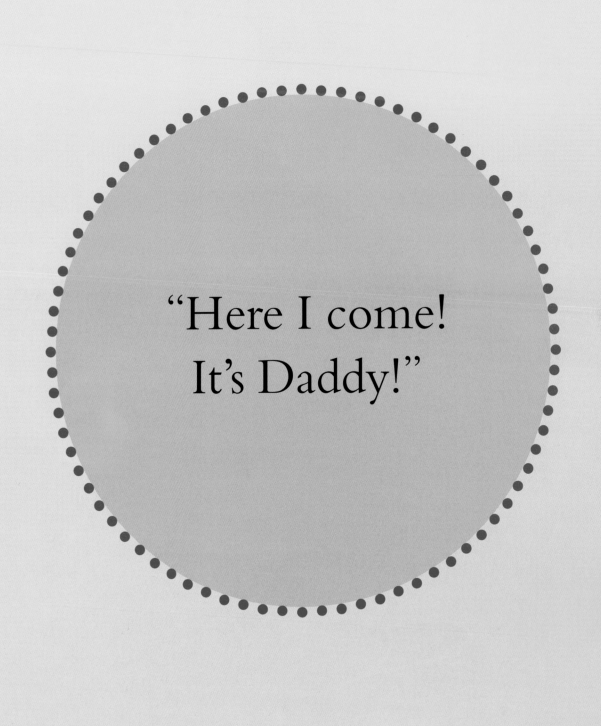

"Here I come!
It's Daddy!"

one

"I'm so glad you're my baby!" hug

*

1

two
teeny, tiny
finger hugs

* *

2

three

pat and burp
the baby hugs

* * *

3

five

"Kiss it all better" boo-boo hugs

* * * * *

5

seven

peekaboo
pajama hugs

* * * * * * *

7

eight

dancing on Daddy's feet cha-cha hugs

* * * * * * * * *

8

ten

"I love you, I love you,
I love you, I love you,
I love you, I love you,
I love you, I love you,
I love you, I love you!"
good-night hugs

* * * * * * * * * *

10

Good night!